P9-AQN-691

The Queen Who Saved Her People

DISCARDED

Tilda Balsley

illustrated by
Ilene Richard

KAR-BEN
PUBLISHING

For Sarah and Heather—the wonderful women who
completed our family —T.B.

For my parents, my husband Lawrence, my children Jodi
and Corey, and my Corgi Bessie —I.R.

Text copyright © 2011 by Tilda Balsley
Illustrations copyright © 2011 by Lerner Publishing Group, Inc.

All rights reserved. International copyright secured. No part of this book may
be reproduced, stored in a retrieval system, or transmitted in any form or
by any means—electronic, mechanical, photocopying, recording, or otherwise—
without the written permission of Lerner Publishing Group, Inc., except for the
inclusion of brief quotations in an acknowledged review.

Kar-Ben Publishing
A division of Lerner Publishing Group, Inc.
241 First Avenue North
Minneapolis, MN 55401 USA
1-800-4KARBEN

Website address: www.karben.com

Library of Congress Cataloging-in-Publication Data

Balsley, Tilda.
    The queen who saved her people / by Tilda Balsley ; illustrated by Ilene Richard.
        p.   cm.
    ISBN 978-0-7613-5093-4 (pbk. : alk. paper)
    ISBN 978-0-7613-7200-4 (EB pdf)
    1. Esther, Queen of Persia—Juvenile literature. 2. Bible stories, English—O.T. Esther. 3. Bible plays,
American. I. Richard, Ilene. II. Title.
    BS580.E8B35 2011
    222'.909505—dc22   2010043815

Manufactured in the United States of America
3 - DOC - 1/1/16

For more Purim fun, this story may be performed as a Readers Theater script. You can assign five parts:

NARRATOR—read the text in **BLACK TYPE.**

KING AHASHUERUS—read the text in **GREEN TYPE.**

QUEEN ESTHER—read the text in **PURPLE TYPE.**

MORDECHAI—read the text in **BLUE TYPE.**

HAMAN—read the text in **RED TYPE.**

Bring young ladies sweet and fair,
But only when you've fixed their hair,
Put perfume here and perfume there,
Given them clean underwear,
And treated them to free health care.

I NEED A QUEEN! LOOK EVERYWHERE!

Beside the palace lived a Jew.
This Mordechai was strong and true.
His cousin Esther lived there, too.
The king's men saw her—all agreed
He'd like this lady—guaranteed.

Her cousin hugged and kissed her twice.
And whispered quickly this advice:

She didn't tell, nobody guessed.
The King met her and was impressed.

Her cousin was around a lot.
One day he overheard a plot.
Death to the King? He was distraught.
He warned the Queen.
The men were caught.

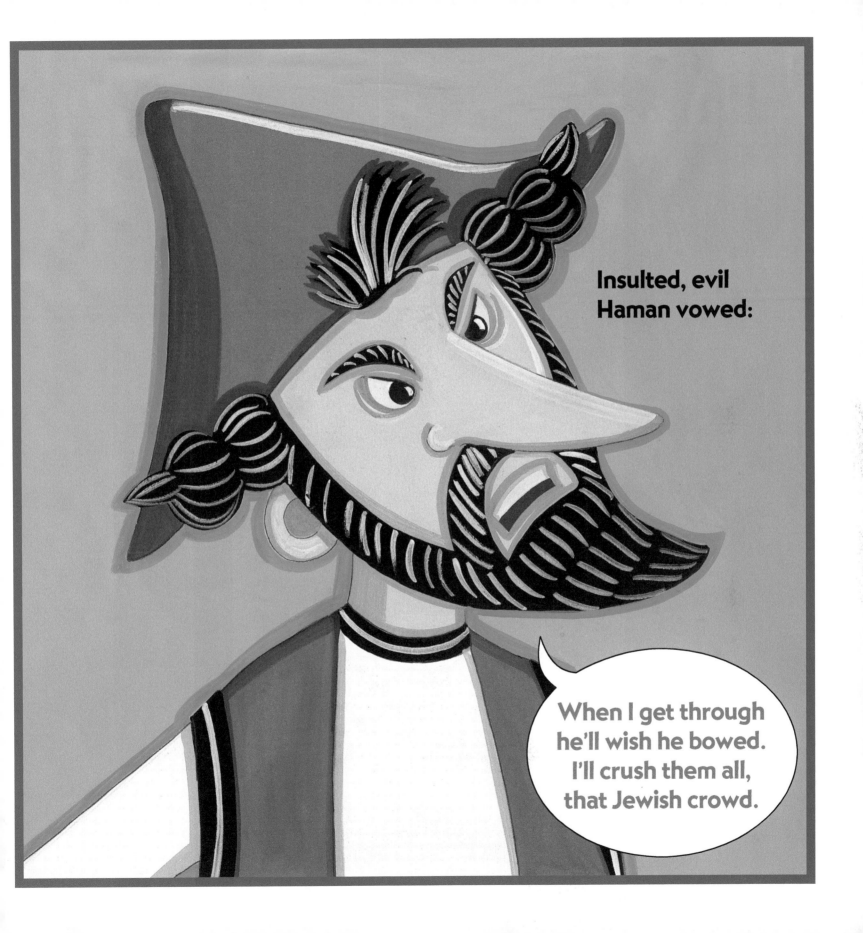

A lot (or *pur*) helped set the date
For Haman's plan. He couldn't wait.

So Mordechai put sackcloth on.
The sounds of grief were loud and long.
The Queen said:

Something's very wrong.
Please explain this, Mordechai.
The whole megillah,
what and why.

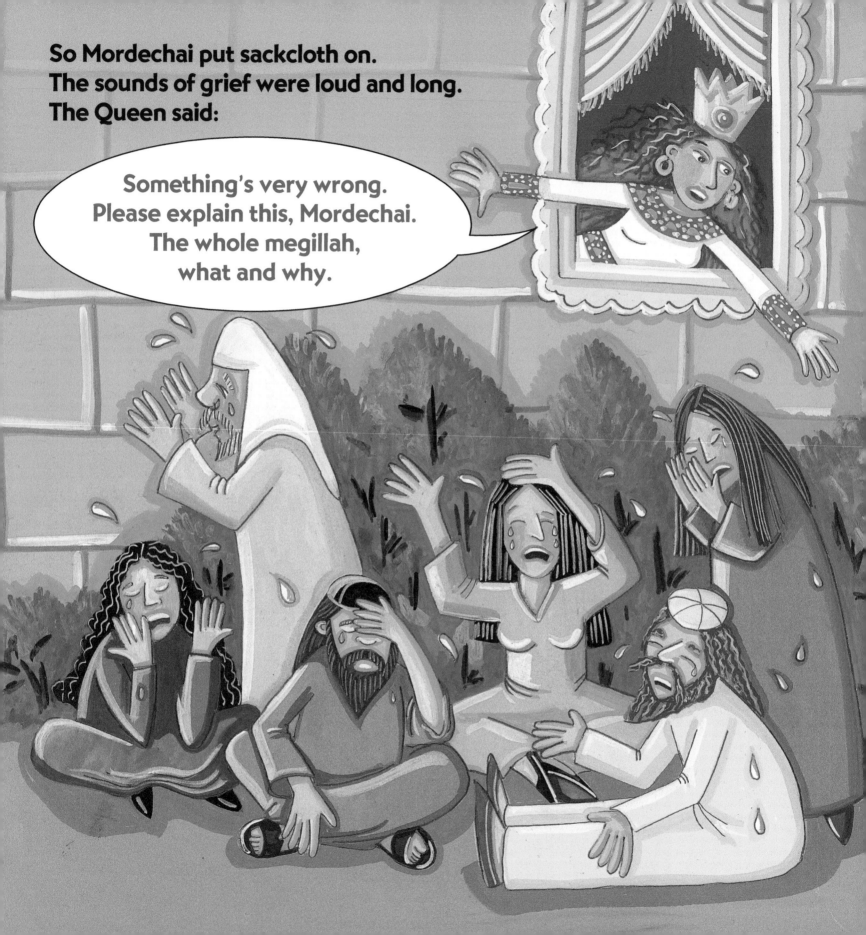

Haman is a dangerous man.
He's put in place an evil plan.
Your people need you. Beg the King,
For only he can fix this thing.

The Queen said:
Me? Beseech the King?
I cannot ask him anything.
It's death for those who dare to go,
Unless invited. You should know.

The King, at dinner, asked once more:

As Haman left, his mood was great
Until he saw parked at the gate

Mordechai, the Jew I hate!

His wife said,
"Build a gallows high."

At his palace, curtain drawn,
The restless King, still up at dawn,
Flipped through his journal with a yawn.

Hmm… Mordechai…. What does this say?
It seems he saved my life one day.
Did we declare a holiday?
Give him a little bonus pay?
A silver medal, anyway?

Now guess who just then happened by
To say, "Let's hang this Mordechai."
The King invited Haman in,
And Haman smiled his wicked grin.

Haman, tell me how I ought
To honor someone.
What's your thought?

And Haman, sure he was the man,
Laid out a very special plan.

A royal horse
with royal crown.
A royal escort
through the town.

So Haman had no choice, of course.
His rival rode the royal horse.

Meanwhile, Esther cooked for three.
The dinner party seemed carefree.
But then the brave Queen snuggled near
And whispered in her husband's ear.

My people live in deathly fear
And only you can help, it's clear.

What? My Esther, tell me who
Has dared to threaten all of you?

He's with us now, still drinking wine,
He is no friend of yours or mine.

Now the tables had been turned
Jews enjoyed a peace, hard-earned.
For following the King's command.
No enemy was left to stand.
And Mordechai, the king's right hand
Sent this message through the land:

Let every
generation read
How on these days the
Jews were freed,
Through Esther's brave
and selfless deed.
Let there be time
for joy and laughter,
At Purim now –
and ever after.